Psst...
Tash is ...

C. McDonald p

# Hold Me

CHELSEA McDONALD

# CHAPTER ONE
## Natasha

"What are you upset for, nooooooow?" Gabby groans as soon as she answers the phone. She doesn't even give me the benefit of the doubt. I could be in the best mood ever, she doesn't know. She wouldn't know because the bitch moved out, basically ending our friendship forever. I mean, she's right I am calling because I'm upset. I'm having serious withdrawals of my best friend, that entitles me to ring her whenever I please and however much I please.

"My roommate just moved out to live with her stupid hunk of a boyfriend. Of course, I'm upset! What am I going to do without you, Gabby? I hate living alone, it's always too quiet and everything echoes when you're on your own." I whine childishly. I'm happy for her but that doesn't mean I want her to go off and leave me forever. By far she's been the best roommate I've ever had. We've grown so close. When I advertised for a roommate I didn't realise I'd get a lifelong best friend as well.

"It's been a week already. You're still alive, you're going to be fine. Plus, we've already started looking for your replacement roommate. They'll never be as awesome as I am, I know, but I'm sure we can still find you someone half decent."

"I don't want anyone else. What if they turn out to be axe murderers? Gabby, what if they're cannibals!"

"Oh, I bet you'd taste delicious. You eat fancy food all the time, not to mention you'd have none of that horrible chewy fat on you."

"Okay, seriously? You're not helping."

"Babe, I don't know what else you want me to say. I promise, we'll find you someone that's not completely whacko and you'll be fine. Just watch. In fact, to go the extra mile, I'll ask around and see if Ellie or Kate know anyone that's looking."

"That's a much better pep talk. Thank you, I'd appreciate that."

"Okay, I've gotta go now. I'm at work until four, I

love bank holidays. But, I'm sure I'll speak to you again later tonight."

"I'll talk to you then."

I flop back onto the bed and groan. I've got work tonight. Unfortunately, not everywhere closes early just because it's a bank holiday. Such as restaurants, they do not. Which means no extra time off for me.

I suppose working isn't that big of a chore when you've literally got nothing else to do and nowhere else to go. Plus, my job isn't hard. I'm one of the top chefs in the county, so I know I'm good at what I do. I'm just glad the skill comes naturally, otherwise, I'd be screwed.

I flick on the telly, settling on my favourite show; F.R.I.E.N.D.S. I like the background noise even if I don't actually plan on watching it.

I run the tap for a bath. I hope a nice steamy bath will help calm my nerves. It's not that I'm scared to live alone, I just don't like it. Coming into an empty house makes me feel like I missed the zombie apocalypse, and so I'm left to wander the Earth on my own. It's why I'm desperate for a replacement roommate. I don't hold out any high hopes, I definitely won't get as lucky as last time when I scored Gabby. But, a decent human being would be okay, even if they were just to keep the lights on and eat all my food.

I sink into the tub of warm bubbles as I listen to Joey try to pick up some chick at Central Perk. Of course, he'll succeed, sleep with her and then completely forget about her as if the whole ordeal never even happened. Been there, felt that.

I know another reason I don't wanna live alone is because it reminds me just how empty my life really is. Yeah, I've got a good job, and so maybe I have a couple of friends. But that's it. Empty. I don't hold a lot of stock in having to be in a relationship. But it would be nice. I sometimes fantasize about walking through the front door to see someone cooking me dinner, it would be horrible but the gesture would mean everything to me. It's been such a long time since I've had that. Almost four years.

Cricket, his name was. I don't even remember the backstory behind that one.

Maybe it's time that I shift my focus from guys to something else. I could get a hobby. Or, even better, I could get a cat. I startle myself with the brilliance of my newly thought up idea. Yep, my mind is made up. I'm going to get myself a cat. Although, that will affect the number of applicants I'll get for Gabby's old room. Or, just maybe, it'll weed out the psychos. The only people that hate cats are strange people, right?

Game, set and match. Ooh, I suddenly feel giddy.

There's a pet shelter basically on my way to work if I go the long way and then make three wrong turns. It feels like it was meant to be. Why the hell hadn't I thought of this sooner?

I jump out of the bath and quickly rush to get ready. The sooner I get there the more time I'll have to spend picking out the right one.

My shift dragged by annoyingly slow last night. I think it was because I was checking the clock every two minutes, counting down the hours until I could escape. We stop serving food at half ten on weekdays, not even a minute later I was packing up my things and rushing to clock out.

As soon as I got in, I got changed and hopped right into bed. I remember as I kid I'd used to do the same thing on Christmas Eve, go to bed early in the hopes that Santa Claus would come quicker. It works though, this morning I woke up refreshed and excited to start this new chapter of my life. With Whiskey, my new little girl that I'm going to collect this morning.

Dressed in jeans and one of my brother's old hoodies I jump in my car. And this is exactly why I have a car. You just never know when you may need it to haul a car-load of cat crap around. I head to Walmart first. I did some research and cat's need a lot of stuff.

I grab a trolley and make my way straight over to the pet aisle. Even looking at the aisle is daunting. There's so many choices, do we really need that many options of cat food. But as I start reading labels I see that they've all got different flavours.

Shit! I start panicking because what if Whiskey is allergic to liver? Or what if she doesn't quite like the taste of duck? Oh, this is a nightmare. Is there not a taster pack?

I start scanning the shelves again for a pack that offers more selection. "Is there anything you're looking for in particular? Maybe I can help?"

I don't know why but I let out a massive yelp when I hear the man next to me talk. I turn to look over and *hot dang,* "Do you work here?"

He chuckles, giving me a glimpse of pearly white teeth. "No, but I do have a cat. Is there something you needed?"

He's gorgeous and he owns a cat. *Gay or married?* I slyly glance down, nope, no ring. Tha can only mean one of two things. He's either gay or he's married hiding his marriage from his mistress. Or, he could be a cat-owning alien that comes down to earth trolling for human sacrifices. *Hmm.* I'm not sure yet.

"Um, yeah actually." Fuck, I was staring for way too long, he totally noticed. "This is going to sound silly but do they have a selection pack? I'm getting a cat and I'm not sure what her taste buds are like yet."

He chuckles lightly. I don't understand the joke, is he outraged too that they don't do selection packs? We should write a horrendously worded letter to the company.

"Oh," His face straightens up. "You weren't joking?"

"No..." This really isn't a joking matter. I'm going to bring Whiskey home, and she's going to be allergic to the liver, and she's either going to puff up like a balloon or she's going to starve.

"No, they don't sell selection packs." He smiles like it's acceptable. God, I feel sorry for his one flavour cat. Humans definitely do not eat the same thing, day in and day out. Why the hell would we subject our cats to that kind of mind-numbing lifestyle?

"Rightio." I turn back around to the shelves and start grabbing a bag of each flavour. If the store isn't going to provide a selection bag for my little girl then I'll have to create my own.

"Sorry I couldn't be of more help."

"Oh, it's fine. Thanks anyway."

"I didn't catch your name?"

I decide to throw him a bone, he was at least trying to be helpful. "It's Tash."

"Well, Tash, I don't usually do this but would you like to get a drink sometime?"

My mind gasps in shock.

"Actually, you know what, don't answer that. Here's my card. Call me if you're interested."

"Okay." I nod as I take the card. It reads, Jacob Bartoli. *Oh, god,* insurance salesman. I try not to let the horror show through on my face as he starts backing away.

"I'll see ya around." He calls. I smile and wave. Just like the penguins from Madagascar. As soon as he's out of sight I shove the card in my pocket, already planning on throwing it in the nearest trash can. The man laughed at me. And, he's obviously cruel to his cat. I almost feel like going out with him and following him home just, so I could rescue his poor miserable cat.

# CHAPTER TWO
*Luke*

The sound of my baby nephew wailing pierces my eardrums, reminding me yet again that I need to look for a new place to live. I love Jay to bits, and he played a big part in why I moved in. I wanted to be around to help out my sister, also the fact that I didn't have anywhere to stay, of course, contributed.

Emma and Adam hadn't seemed to mind, there was no doubt that they had the room but I think they were happy to have someone to watch Jay while they took time out for themselves too.

But, this situation isn't working anymore. I started my new job at the vet clinic nearly two weeks ago and I'm positive that I haven't had a full night's sleep since.

Which is why today when I arrive at work I'm late. I called in to say I wasn't coming in until later than usual and of course, they were fine with it but that's not the point. I need sleep and time to relax. After all, it's not my fucking kid.

When lunchtime comes around I settled myself into a chair out in the small courtyard behind the clinic with my coffee, my sandwich, and the classifieds. I've been actively searching for a new place, somewhere local so that I can still pop around to Emma's anytime she needs me, but also far enough away that I won't be able to hear baby cries.

I've inspected four properties so far but there was something wrong with each and every one. And that's not just me being picky, one couple had three kids all under the age of five. Yeah, so not fucking happening.

I'm surprised when Gabby's name lights up my phone screen. Yes! Just what I need right now, a night with my friends. A drink or five couldn't hurt either. It's probably only been a week since I've seen them all but it feels like so much longer.

"Hey Gabby, how's it going?" I'm immediately cheered up and I know that the rest of the day won't be so bad.

"Great actually. I had an idea. Last time we all got

together you were complaining about living with your sister, right?"

"Ugh, Gabs don't make me sound like such a jerk. I appreciate everything she and Adam have done for me, letting me live here and all. I just happened to mention looking for somewhere more suited for me, more appropriate that's all."

"I know, I know. But, I may have a solution for you." She pauses.

I wait silently for her to continue. When she doesn't I jump in with, "and what would that be?"

"I've recently vacated Tashs' apartment, which means she has a spare room. As far as I know, she hasn't rented it out yet."

"Tash?" Hmm. I've only met her a handful of times, she seemed nice.

Of course, I've already violated her in my mind six ways to Sunday. She's not my usual type, she's cute and petite - like a fairy. I'd never make a move because I know how much she means to Gabby. And Gabby would kill me if I did my usual play with her.

Could I really live with someone I'm attracted to? *Pfft, hell yeah.*

"I'm going to invite her out for drinks with us on Thursday night. Maybe try and talk to her then, get to know her a little bit."

I sigh but reluctantly agree. It's the least I could do. "Fine."

"Honestly, you'd be lucky to score such a sweet roommate." She doesn't have to hammer it home; the fact is I'm desperate and as long as she's sane I'm interested. Apart from cannibalism there's not much I wouldn't put up with. I keep myself to myself, and what they get up to isn't any of my business.

To talk to my sister and her husband, I decided I'd do it over dinner. I'm not the best chef in the world, I know that for sure but I think I do okay. I make a very plain spaghetti bolognese and set out the plates.

"I've got something I wanted to talk to you guys about," I edge.

"Have you been dating someone? Because I was talking to mom the other day, and she asked me the same thing. And I had a feeling. I mean I know, absolutely, you're only young and of course, you don't need to worry about settling down or anything just yet."

"But, well, if you did then that'd be great, it would really take all the heat of off us." Adam rushes exhaustedly. *Wow*. I always knew my sister was crazy but it's seemed that her crazy has started to infect Adam.

"Hey, whoa. That's not what this is. I thought I should let you guys know that I'm looking for a new place to live."

"Oh."

"Well, we didn't expect for you to live with us forever."

"It's just been so nice having you around. Not just for Jay, but for me too. I don't think we've been this close since we were kids."

"I just think it's time." I smile gently before taking a sip of water to swallow down the lump in my throat.

"I'll call mom, she'll almost be ready to throw you a going away party." Emma runs off for her mobile while I sit, can't help but feeling a little lost. I breathe deeply as the weight lifts off my chest.

"We're sure going to miss you around here." I barely hear Adam say as my sister squeals down the phone to my mother. I doubt they're still on the subject of me, they've probably shifted to the dress fitting for my cousin's wedding. Or something as equally important.

# CHAPTER THREE

Natasha

"What's up?" I answer Gabby's call.

"I may have a solution for you!" She practically screams in my ear.

"Okay..." Immediately, my interest is piqued. "A solution for which of my problems?"

I have so many. Unfortunately. But I think because I'm aware of my own chaos, it's all going to be okay.

Gabby laughs on the other end of the call. "For the problem, I seem to have created by moving out."

Oh, that one. Yeah, that was a big one right now. I'm rational enough to know that I'll get used to not having my best friend right next door. I've lived alone before, I've had other roommates. Just, it's unlikely that anyone will ever top Gabby. She was the best.

"Ah, yes. Well, since you did create the problem you should definitely be the one to fix it."

"What if I told you that I have a friend looking for a place?"

Hmm. "Depends. Which friend is it?"

I know all of Gabby's close friends, the circle she ran with in college. I've hung out with them a lot since meeting Gabby. Everyone had seemed nice enough. But, I hadn't realised anyone was looking for a room to rent.

I hear a change in Gabby's breathing. Either Sam has his hands on her or she's about to annoy me.

"Well, you've met him..."

"Whoa, whoa. Hold your horses there, buddy." I inhale deeply and exhale calmly. "Him?"

"Yeah, that's kind of the only thin-"

"Gabbbbbbby," I whine exaggeratedly. "You know what happened with my last male roommate! I'm sorry but I really don't want a repeat of that experience. Or the male-mate before that, or even the one before that."

"What happened with that last one you mentioned?"

"Which one? One, two or three?"

"The very first one. I don't know if I remember this story."

"He was the one from the cult? He tried to cut my

hair in the middle of the night? I still swear he was going to use it for a love spell."

"What a freak!"

"I really don't know if I could handle another male-mate Gabby." I sigh restlessly. I've had my own place since I was nineteen, nine years ago. Throughout that whole time, I've never been on my own for long. I liked the company, even if it was just someone to say hello to in the mornings. But, I've had some real nutcases, which is why I hate the thought of another male roommate.

In total, I've had eleven roommates, plus Gabby equals twelve. Out of all those people, I probably only really liked three of them. I tolerated three of them and I hated the other five.

I had to move after my first male-mate. There was no way in hell I wanted that crazy knowing where I lived. I've also had a crazy-jealous girlfriend that thought I was trying to steal her boyfriend, a guy that walked around completely naked, and a chick that used my closet and vanity as her personal department store. The last guy I had living with me was the second to last roommate before Gabby.

Now, he wasn't completely alien, just an absolute filth bag. He was good-looking, clean and a charmer. The only real problem was that maybe he was too charming. Every night he'd bring a different girl home. I'm not a prude and I'm certainly not anyone's mother. You fuck who you wanna fuck. But when it gets to the point of sleepless nights and walking in on a threesome on my perfectly nice couch, I had to draw the line.

Even the notion of having another male roommate makes me queasy. But now that I'm thinking about it, is it weird that I've never lived with a boyfriend? Counting back all my past relationships, I've never gone past giving them a key. I've never had the desire to constantly be that close to someone I was dating.

A thought occurs to me, "you said I know him? Who is it?"

"It's... Luke."

"You know he's been living with his sister and brother-in-law. I think he's going a bit crazy with the baby and all that fuss. He said he was looking for a new place the last time I saw him."

"Tash?"

"Yeah, I'm here."

"Look, I know he's a guy but I can guarantee that he won't be like your other roommates. Plus, you've met him, you've seen with your own eyes that he's a normal human being."

"I suppose..."

"How about we get the whole gang together at the

bar? It's a relaxed setting for you to suss him out a bit more. Ask him about any annoying traits, and I bet Evan will have some stories for you. They used to room together in college, he'll know all the dirty details. Hmm?"

She makes a very convincing point, it's a very compelling part of her nature. She really could've been a lawyer, but I suppose if you were after anyone to teach your kids manners and good behaviour, you'd want Gabby.

"Fine. But if I decide to drop him from the male-mate candidate ballot then you have to drop it too. Deal?"

"Deal." She agrees far too quickly for my liking.

"Meet you at Lanes at 6?"

I agree and hang up the phone. I guess if things go south, at the very least I'll have a chance to thoroughly investigate Luke tonight.

WHEN I ARRIVE at the bar later on that afternoon, I see that Gabby isn't here yet. I have no doubt Gabby will be bringing Sam tonight, the big guy barely ever leaves her side. And, he's most definitely the reason Gabby is late. They're more like dogs in heat than fully grown humans. But I secretly admire their sheer lack of self-control, in the weirdest of ways, it's sweet.

I don't even need to look around anymore, I already know we'll be seated in their usual booth. As I walk over I see Luke tucked between Kate and Ellie wearing that stupid hat. I've met him like a dozen times, and every single time he's wearing a hat. I wonder what colour his hair is? There must be something seriously wrong with it if it always needs covering up.

Maybe it's where he stashes his condoms. I've heard repeatedly how much of a playboy he is or at least was before he moved in with his sister. That must be why he wants to move, so he can start hooking up with randoms again. I can't help my internal groan; I knew this was a bad idea.

Should I turn back? Call Gabby saying I don't feel well, I'm sure she'd be fine with it. But, I know it wouldn't be long until she was back on my case. This wasn't something she seemed likely to drop easily.

"Tash!" Kate calls, unknowingly deciding my fate.

"Hey." I smile and move swiftly to take the seat next to her. They're joking on, sounds like it's about Evan and Ellie living together. I didn't have any siblings but seeing them together kinda made me wish I did. As far as twins go, they may not look much alike, but they're as close as can be. I smile and nod hello to everyone before pulling my coat off.

"What's it like bringing lays back to the apartment? Do you have to ask permission?" Luke roasts.

"Do you have to hang a sock on the door?" Kate chuckles along. I grin watching their reactions. Ellie is joining in on the laughter, Evan, on the other hand, is blushing. Aww.

"Alright, alright. I wanna be anywhere but here right now. Tash, would you like a drink?"

I'm not much of a drinker but I take pity on him, "Rum and coke please."

Luke boos as Evan stands and walks to the bar.

"Oh, don't worry about him," Ellie says before turning and swatting at Luke. "And to answer your insanely rude question Luke. Nothing like that has happened, yet. Thank god."

"Aww is little El going through a dry spell?" I watch as he stretches his arm around her shoulders. "Need me to help you out, babe?"

Kate shakes with loud laughter as Ellie shivers and shoves Luke's arm away from her. "In your dreams. What you gonna do? Take me back to your sister's house. Thanks, but hell to the no, thanks."

Even I can't hold back my giggles when Luke responds with an overly cheesy wink.

Evan returns with my drink and another beer and I'm quick to thank him. Kate's fiddling on her phone before sighing out loud.

"What's wrong?" I ask her.

"Gabby texted. She and Sam won't be able to make it. Something's come up." Kate rolls her eyes. We all know what that means.

"Nice choice of words," I remark, sipping on my drink.

"Well, at least we know Gabby's getting looked after. El, you ever want the same treatment you let me know." Luke jokes, to which he receives a hearty push from Ellie.

"Dude!" Evan says shaking his head.

"So Tash, how's it going? The restaurant been busy?" Ellie asks directing the attention somewhere else, apparently in my direction.

"Always." I laugh. There is literally never a time when it's not busy, which is one of the things I love about my job. I don't know how I'd cope if I were in another line of work. After climbing the ladder all these years, I'm now at the top of my field in a four-and-a-half-star restaurant. The better the restaurant, the busier you are. I love it.

"I'd do absolutely anything to get a table at *Unleash*." Ellie groans dramatically.

"Well, why didn't you say so?" I may only be the chef but I can still pull a few strings. I've never had the desire to dine there but I think that's just because it's my place of work. The restaurant is truly stunning and of course, the food is to die for.

Ellie's eyes almost fall out of her head, she almost looks like a cartoon. "For real?"

"Dude, she's the head chef. Why don't you just ask her to come around and cook you dinner." Kate pokes fun at her friend, throwing her head back as she laughs.

My throat itches and I clear it awkwardly. "Well, one of them." Unfortunately, I have to share that title with three other people, so that there's always someone there to run the kitchen. "But text me and let me know when, yeah?"

"Oh definitely!"

"Does that offer apply to us too?" Evan jibes flirtatiously. He's being more sociable than normal tonight and I'm starting to wonder if it has anything to do with the death stares Kate's been secretly shooting him all night. Oh, yeah, I noticed that, Kate. Apparently, she's not as sly as she seems, or maybe it's the way she's downing her drinks that's causing her to get sloppier.

I haven't known these guys very long but I felt the vibe between Kate and Evan a long time ago. And I'm guessing that if I can tell they're acting weird tonight, everyone else can too. I can only imagine the grilling Evans going to get off of Ellie.

"Of course." I smile nonchalantly. Evan's cute and if I'd met him on his own, maybe in a supermarket somewhere, I'd totally be interested. But that boy has Kate's name stamped all over him. And while I know Kate can be as sweet as pie, I've heard the stories - she goes from zero to scorned lioness in approximately zero point three two seconds.

Besides, I wouldn't ever want to stand in the way of true love.

"Does anyone want anything?" Luke rattles around his empty bottle. "I need another."

I'm still working on mine. I highly doubt I get another drink at all but Kate downs the rest of the pink liquid in her glass and raises it to Luke. He takes it as he squeezes past Ellie and Evan.

"Wait, Tash. Gabby mentioned that you had a spare room since she moved out. You know that'd be perfect for-"

It must be the alcohol flowing through my body that makes me jump up and shove my hand over her mouth. "Shhhhhhhh."

"Why 'shh'?" Evan asks while Ellie and Kate just stare at me like I've lost my marbles. Which as I slowly start to look at my position, I might have.

Evan laughs and I right myself, slipping back into my seat. I shrug apologetically at Ellie, "Sorry."

"I'm not sure if Luke knows. I actually wanted to ask you about living with him first. Gabby mentioned that you shared a dorm in college." I look pointedly at Evan.

I'm surprised when all three bodies burst with laughter. Well shit, that can't be good. He must've been a real nightmare in college!

"He wasn't *that* bad." Evan calms down first but the way he says 'that' does nothing to sooth my unease. Yeah, I'm definitely not convinced. "Look, I promise, you'll be fine. He was a bit wild back then, but he's calmed down a lot since."

I level him with a stare before looking sceptically between Kate and Ellie. "He's a bit boisterous, but he's no harm, honestly, he'd make a good roommate for you."

Luke returns to the table with drinks and settles himself next to Evan on the edge of the booth. Right across from me. It's very distracting. I've got to admit, he may not be my type, but he sure is unnervingly gorgeous, even with his stupid cap.

His clothes aren't fancy but the way he pulls them off, you'd think they were designer. Maybe they are, how the hell would I know? He's got on a white tee with an unbuttoned denim shirt over it. His sleeves are pushed up to the elbows, revealing his smooth flawless skin and his fair arm hair.

I try my best to keep my glances on the down-low but I'm curious. I want to study him, see more of him. If only he'd take that damn hat off, then I'd be able to see the whole picture. Glimpse the colour of his eyes, finally see if his hair matches the fair hair from his arms.

I slowly sip the rest of my drink as the group continues to chatter away. I decide that I'll leave after my drink. I came, I got the information I needed, now all I have to do is think it over. I look around as the noise around us becomes louder, where has the time gone?

I bid my goodbyes, claiming I have an early start in the morning. While Kate's drastically sad that I'm leaving, I suspect she's feeling the wonderful effects of her fruity cocktails, everyone else understands. It's not really lying when I fully expect Gabby to call in the morning, apologize for not being here and then demand my answer about Luke.

The more I sat there with the hot male-mate candidate, the more I couldn't think straight. Better to leave now than later.

When I arrive home it's quiet. I flick the lights on

and make my way to my bedroom. I spot Whiskey's furry body in the middle of my bed. Great, even my cat's not bothered about spending time with me.

The longer I sit alone in the silence the more it cements in just how much I need a roommate. And while I don't necessarily like Luke, I trust my new friends with their opinions.

# CHAPTER FOUR

Luke

I raise my fist and rap my knuckles against the apartment door. I hear the locks moving on the other side of the door before it's swung open.

"Hey." Tash smiles and suddenly I'm finding myself less apprehensive about this whole arrangement. This hadn't been anywhere near what I had in mind when I decided I wanted to find a new place to live. When Gabby suggested it, she made it annoyingly difficult to argue with her. I didn't have a leg to stand on, the rent is cheap, it's a nice enough area - close to work. I couldn't exactly tell Gabby that I didn't want to move in with Tash because I found her attractive.

To me, living with someone you're attracted to but not being able to do anything, reeked of bad luck. And blue balls. But if I'd told Gabby that, she'd have been over the moon and start playing matchmaker. But I didn't need help, if I wanted Tash - or any girl - that badly, I'd find a way to charm them.

"I'm so sorry, come in." The pixie in front of me pulls the door open wider. I pick up my boxes from where they were resting on the floor and enter the apartment. Tash closes the door with a quizzical look set on her face. "Is that all your stuff?"

"Yeah, I like travelling light."

"Okaaaaay. I didn't realise people actually did that but to each their own." Her reply makes my eyes wander. She leads me through the entryway and into a main living area. I see what she means now. The couch is completely covered with throw blankets and cushions. So much so that I can't tell what colour the couch actually is. Knick-knacks and photographs line all the surfaces. But instead of feeling cluttered, it's homely. Comfy.

I peek my head around the corner into the adjoining room. It's a large kitchen that's decked out and immaculately clean. I wonder if my new roommate, the five-star chef, cooks at home. I suppose if I spent all day at work cooking, I wouldn't want to then come home and cook some more. My dreams of restaurant quality food and leftovers die on the spot.

"Oh, I forgot to ask if you were okay with cats. Well, I assume you are otherwise Gabby wouldn't have made the arrangements." She moves over to a ginger furball taking up residence on one of the armchairs.

Which is exactly what Gabby did, made arrangements. Yet again, pulling on the strings of all her puppets commanding them to dance. I mentally sigh because it's a bit late to back out of this whole ordeal now, as I stand in Tashs' living room with my duffle and a handful of boxes in tow.

"I'm a vet. So, to answer your non-existent question, no, I don't mind cats." I watch her face carefully as she tries to hide her surprise. Yeah, class clown Luke actually has a proper job. I should be insulted but I get that reaction a lot, more times than I'd care to admit. Tells me a lot about what people see when they look at me.

"Oh wow, that's handy. Well, this here is Whiskey. I only got her last week, but we've become fast friends. Haven't we girl?" She continues scratching behind the cats' ears causing Whiskey to purr.

"Girl? And you named *her,* Whiskey?"

"Yeah. You got a problem with her name?" She jumps up from the floor armed with a raised eyebrow looking ready to go twelve rounds. Wow. She's a feisty little pixie. I have to admit I didn't see that one coming.

And look at me judging someone on looks alone - just the thing I hate.

"No, ma'am. So, uhh, where's the bedroom?" I shift the boxes in my arms again, as if just remembering they're still there.

"Oh crap, sorry! I got distracted. You'll probably notice that I do that a lot, and no, it's not an annoying habit. It's an adorable feature." She bounces past me and leads the way down the hall. She stops at the door on the left and pushes it open. "This one's yours. That window overlooks the west, it has an en-suite attached, and I hope you don't mind that it's furnished. I already had most of it, but Gabby left a few bits as well. Whatever you don't want just let me know and I'll get rid of it for you. Although..." She inspects my three boxes pointedly, "I'm guessing you'll want the furniture left where it is if that's all you've got.."

"Yeah, that's awesome. Gabby had mentioned you had furniture. Is there anything else I should know? Any alarm codes or house rules of sorts?"

"Well, now that you mention it, yes. The alarm code is two-seven-seven-four. But on another note, keep your shit tidy, don't be keeping me awake all night, don't be a TV hog, no drugs, no wild parties, be nice to Whiskey and never, ever leave my kitchen a mess. Got it?"

"Wow, it's like living with mum and dad all over again." I joke.

She ignores me and continues on with her rampant little speech. Is it weird that I'm mildly aroused right now? "The perks of being my roommate; I keep my shit tidy, I'm usually asleep by 10 when I'm not at work. I will only really use the TV in the living room for the music channels or for movie marathons. Also, I don't do drugs, I'm not a partier, I work most nights as a chef. I'll often experiment cooking new dishes at home before I add them to the menu at work so there is literally always food in the kitchen, which you are free to help yourself to."

She releases a giant breath, "I've probably told you more about myself in those three minutes than I would on the first five dates with someone. Any questions?"

"No. I'm pretty sure you've covered everything I could possibly, ever, want to know." I set my boxes down on the bed and turn back around to face her.

"Okay, I'll leave you to get settled. If you need help unpacking, you should probably call someone else. I'm making pasta for tea." She calls out, already halfway down the hallway. I'm hanging onto the door frame as I watch her hips sway. When she's out of sight I retreat into my new room and close the bedroom door.

This is going to be harder than I thought. I'd heard

Gabby talk about Tash, but only snippets. Evidently, snippets I wasn't really paying attention to. And, despite hanging out with her with the group, I didn't really know anything about her. She was quiet, or maybe I just wasn't paying as much attention as I should have been. Clearly.

She seemed to get on well with the girls last night. But now that I think about it, I recall seeing a photo of her with Gabby and Kate a while ago. So maybe that was it, she'd had bonus time to bond with them.

I want to bang my head against a wall but I'm afraid the noise would draw Tashs' attention. All those times I'd met her before she was just Gabby's hot friend. She'd immediately been marked as off limits because I couldn't trust myself not to screw up their friendship. All those times I'd kept my distance, I'd done the right thing - the good guy thing. So why did it feel so wrong that I hadn't been paying attention to her?

Now...well now she's my roommate, where does that leave us? Friends? Acquaintances? Roommates who avoid each other because one of them wants to fuck the other? I have no idea.

I pull out my phone, dial Gabby's number and wait for her to answer. She's got to have an answer. She did this, she needs to fix it. "Hey, Luke! What's going on?"

I shoulder the phone to my ear as I start to unpack. I don't have much in a way of clothes and possessions so it's rather easy. Clothes go in the drawers; charger goes on the nightstand and toiletries in the bathroom.

"Are you for real? You want me to live with this chick?" I exclaim before thinking better of it. Well shit, that didn't come out how I meant it to.

"Luke, that's not nice! You haven't even given her a chance. Are you even there yet? And that is one of my best friends you're talking about, by the way." Ooh, she's pissed. Rightly so, I sound like a complete tool.

"Obviously, you're taking what I'm saying the wrong way. Gabs, she's going to drive me nuts. Like, in the best possible way though. She's carefree, she fucking cooks, she has a cat named Whiskey for fuck's sake. Do not even get me started on her ass. Gabby, I've never been so hard from looking at someone in my entire life. That's including high school!"

"Gross. Way too much information there Luke. But, I'm glad you seem to be getting along."

"Gabby are you even listening to the words I'm saying; I don't want to get along with her. I want to be getting it on with her." I sigh already exhausted. "The way she just talked to me, and that feisty sparkle in her eye... why hasn't she ever been like that before?"

"I heard you. Tash, she's just a little shyer in

public. She's a real homebody, right now you're in her comfort zone, of course, she's going to be herself. And all I'd like to say is, check and mate."

"What? Did you set this up?"

"Of course, how else am I going to win the bet. You have no idea how long I've been planning this. And, look how my plan's turning out. First day and you're already majorly crushing on her. Personally, I thought it'd take longer than that."

"THERE'S A BET!" What the hell is happening right now? Shit. I think my heart stops beating. I hold my breath as I listen for movement in the hallway. Nothing. Maybe she didn't hear me.

"Yep, on who can hook you up first. And I am going for gold baby."

"Ugh," I groan. "What the hell do you win?"

"Bragging rights, obviously and two hundred dollars."

"I really can't believe this." My own friends betting on my love life. On any other day, I'd say they should know better but I fear Gabby may have a real chance here.

"Well, believe it. Look, I gotta go. You enjoy your carbonara." *Carbonara?*

"What how did you kn-" And she hung up. *Fan-*

*fucking-tastic.* I'm guessing she planted that little seed as well.

I need a game plan. It's not that I'm against being set up, it's not even that I don't want to be set up with Tash. But, if something were to happen between us, I'd want it to happen naturally - not because it was forced. And, if that did happen, then I would proceed to tell her about the bet that our moronic friends have going.

First things firsts, I need to taste the carbonara my little pixie is making.

# CHAPTER FIVE

So far, so good. It's only been a week, and I've only really seen Luke in passing but it's run smoothly. I picked up a few extra shifts at the restaurant this week which is why when Luke gets home from work every night at half five, I'm already out.

It's actually kind of bummed me out. I had wanted to spend time with him this week. Welcome him properly to the apartment and even get to know him a bit better. I realise now that my initial impression of Luke was way off. He's not that bad at all. So far, he's been clean and quiet. He's even fed Whiskey and cleaned her litter tray when I haven't been home.

It's Thursday afternoon, my first day off since Luke

moved in. I send him a text asking if he has any plans tonight, which he replies immediately to.

*No. Are you at work tonight? - Luke*
*Nope. Want to hang out tonight? - Tash*
*Are you cooking? - Luke*
*Of course - Tash*
*I'll be there ;) - Luke*

I think over his texts and an unknown warmth fills my belly. I like the fact that he likes my cooking. But I'm a chef so it isn't unusual for people to like my food. I'm sure it's a normal thing to seek approval though because really who doesn't want that?

As it's already three in the afternoon, I start prepping the kitchen for a feast. I didn't ask what Luke wanted because I'm not that desperate to feel like a 1950's housewife. I haven't done a roast in a while, but that means I'll need to go shopping. I forgo that idea when I look down, I'm still in my pyjamas. I quickly decide it's going to be that kind of day, which in my mind, equals a pizza party.

I root around the kitchen for all my ingredients. When I notice how little I have in the way of food, I start adding to my grocery list. I'll have to make a trip to the store this weekend. That thought excites me and motivates me as I roll out some fresh dough.

I'm sitting on the couch with Whiskey when Luke

comes through the door. "Pizza's in the oven, shouldn't be too long. Cookies are on the bench."

"Well, hello to you too, stranger." His voice, like velvet. His words, like liquid charm being poured all over me. My spine straightens, my hand that was previously petting Whiskey stills and hovers uselessly in the air.

It hits me how comfortable it feels having Luke live here. I may not have seen him that much this week but his presence has still been noticed. And I like it. He's different than all my other roommates, he makes the place feel warm. Plus, hands down, he smells the best.

Whiskey nudges her wet nose against my fingertips and I resume the motions of stroking her fur. Luke comes in and plops himself down at the other end of the sofa. "How was work?"

"Fine, except that one of the receptionists had to bring her grandmother in with her Pomeranian. Honestly, it doesn't look good for the little fella."

"Poor woman. One of the downsides to pets, they don't live as long as we do."

"What we doing tonight then?"

"Just thought we could hang out, watch a movie, talk? We haven't really seen each other that much, I'm curious to know more about who I'm living with."

"Well, what is it that you wanna know? I'm an open book, ask me anything."

"Ok, I've got one. When Evan said that you were wild in college but you calmed down since then. What did he really mean?"

"I slept around a lot, partied a lot, drank a lot. But he's right, I've changed since then."

"Why?"

"I think it had a lot to do with spending the summer with a girl I really didn't like, but it was my own fault for leading her on. Then, of course, coming back home to live with my sister and her husband." I watch him as he visibly relaxes even further into his seat, "It's been a nice change of pace."

Yeah, I bet. Despite sometimes having the T.V. on, this place is usually pretty quiet. Plus, he's free to do as he pleases here, not that he couldn't at his sisters, but my guess is that bringing chicks back to your sister's house isn't the biggest turn on in the world. Then again, my brother is eight years younger than me and lives halfway across the country. Safe to say we're not quite as close as Luke and Emma.

"For the sake of our situation, I'm glad you've calmed down."

"Since you asked me a question do I get one too?"

"I don't see what harm it could do."

"Does Tash stand for anything? I've never heard you be called by anything else."

"Well actually, my full name is Natasha. But I don't even know if Gabby knows that, so try and keep it on the DL."

"What? Why?" He asks stunned. Then his eyes narrow inquisitively, "Do you not like the name Natasha?"

"It's too long, and it's the only name my parents will call me by - and we don't have that great a relationship."

"Natasha." He stretches it out, playing around with the feel of it on his tongue. He stops abruptly, seemingly to have made a decision. "I like it. Natasha. It's pretty, it suits you."

"I'll let you call me by my full name if you stop wearing those stupid caps. Did you not like, just get off work?" I reach over and snatch the cap off of his head. I'm desperate to know what it is he's hiding under there.

"Stupid? They're not stupid." His hands fly to his golden hair, rapidly trying to fix...I don't know what, his hair is fine. More than that, it's so perfect that I'm conflicted between wanting it for myself and wanting to run my fingers through it.

"Oh yeah they're super dope, with your baggy

pants and chain hanging low. Just do the world a favour, let the caps go." I drop his cap back in his lap.

That's how we continue for the rest of the night. The T.V. plays in the background but neither of us are paying it any attention. We jibe back and forth, we ask questions, we chow down on my amazing pizza. All the while, I can still feel the tingling in my hand, the want to touch him and be closer to him.

ANDREA, one of the other head chefs at work, calls on Friday morning asking to swap my Sunday for her Friday. While I'm sick of work, I agree, so I can get the rest of the weekend off. It's such a relief to know that my shifts revert back to normal next week. But I feel like I need to celebrate my weekend off in some small way. My first thought is to ring Gabby, but she says her and Sam are away on some romantic getaway. She suggests going onto a dating site, yeah because that worked out so well for her. I immediately dismiss the idea.

My next thought is Luke, but I already know he's busy. He told me a few days ago that he'd be out with his mates watching some game.

My uniform sleeve is an inch from catching fire, again, when I pull myself from my daydream.

Maybe Gabby's idea for a date wasn't the most terrible suggestion. Since last night I can't keep my mind away from Luke. The way he said my full name, the way his hair looked - so inviting, testing the strength of my self-control. Yes, a distraction is definitely needed here.

Hmm. That guy from the supermarket springs to mind. I vowed not to go out with him, but he seems like my last resort. Lord only knows where everyone else has disappeared to. Suddenly everyone's got plans and I'm stuck sitting by my lonesome, I don't think so.

After my shift, on the ride home, I decide I'll root around to find supermarket guys business card. I'm sure I hadn't thrown it out. Hopefully, it'll have his name on too, because for the life of me I can't remember it.

SATURDAY MORNING you couldn't drag me from my bed if you paid me. I sleep a few extra hours than I normally do, when I do finally wake up I flick on the TV and spend the next hour lazing. The only reason I contemplate moving from the warmth of my bed is because of the growling beast in my belly.

I sigh out loud. My hunger is winning out over my comfort. I'll have to get something to eat before my stomach gives me a headache with its deafening noises.

"Good morning, sleeping beauty." Luke's voice startles me as I enter the kitchen, it's so quiet I hadn't noticed him sitting at the breakfast bar.

I look over and smile at him, sitting and eating his cereal. It's ridiculous how much I like having someone here to say hello to in the mornings. "Good morning, Luke."

"Why are you so cheery this morning?"

"Hmm. I had a good sleep." I keep my eyes down and focused on pouring my coffee, avoiding any eye contact as I busy myself with making breakfast.

He really doesn't need to know why I had such a good sleep or about the wet dream that woke me up in the middle of the night.

"What have you got planned for today?"

"Oh," I'm about to say that I have a date but I don't yet. I haven't actually rung the guy yet. Jacob, I found his name last night - it's boldly imprinted on the business card that's currently sitting on my bedside table. Of course, even when I do ring Jacob, I'm under no illusion that he'll say yes. He might not remember me, it was a few weeks ago that we met. He could be busy even, but I won't let anything stop me. I'm in such a good mood that today I will be unstoppable.

"Natasha?"

"Sorry. Not much, might run to the grocery store. Is there anything you need?"

"Actually, yeah. As long as you don't mind, I need some Advil."

"Yeah, no problem. I'll add it to the list." I rinse out my cup and leave it on the sink to dry before reaching for my shopping list.

"Are you up to much today?"

"Nope, just going out to watch the game later."

I chuckle stupidly. I knew that. "Right...well, I brought home leftovers from work last night. They're in the fridge, help yourself."

I watch Luke closely as he stands and moves around the island to the sink. His skin brushes against mine as he squeezes by reminding me that I'm not wearing enough clothing to be this close to him.

Or, maybe the problem is that I'm wearing too much. Either way, it freaks me out and I make a mad dash back to my bedroom.

# CHAPTER SIX
*Natasha*

With my bathtub, full and adorned with massive amounts of scented bubbles, I step in for a nice relaxing soak. I love my bathtub but for normal everyday purposes the shower is my go to. Today though is a special occasion, it's date day. As of half an hour ago, I have a date for tonight with supermarket guy. I'm glad I had the sense to close my bedroom door beforehand otherwise there might've been a chance of Luke seeing my happy dance.

Well, it's more of a cross between a sprinkler move and a jump for joy.

The bathroom door swings open startling me out of my thoughts. I turn to look over at a very frozen Luke in the doorway. His eyes travelling up and down my body reminds me that I'm very naked. I squeak and hurry to sink down into the water. It's hot, like really hot but I know I have to endure the pain in hopes that the bubbles will hide my goodies. In my haste to cover up my foot slips, banging my ankle against the tap. I let out a muttered curse as I submerge into the tub.

That fucking hurt. I close my eyes in an attempt to shield myself from the humiliation. I'm such a moron. And a prude. I scatter so hastily to hide myself from Luke when in all truth, I know he's seen everything I've got probably a million times before. It's the twenty-first century, in this day and age there's nothing to hide. Instead of worrying I should've sucked in my tummy and posed. Unfortunately, that's not who I am. Who I am is a very pissed off woman stewing in a boiling hot bath.

What the fuck is he doing in here!

Oh, look I've found my composure - very pissed off persona. As I finally look up, Luke is still stood half in the bathroom half in my bedroom, his hand clutching the doorknob. I raise my eyebrows and clear my throat expectantly. I expect an explanation, and quick.

"I didn't hear you come in," he explains. His eyes are burning into the bubbles that now hide my naked body. After a second he shakes himself and meets my eyes for the first time. "Do you have any Advil? My headache is getting worse."

"GET OUT!" I scream, totally outraged and completely mortified. He spins around and shuts the door but it's too late, the damage is already done. I don't think I've ever been so embarrassed and mad at the same time. I'm not ashamed of my body but I've never been confident enough to just go flashing every Tom, Dick, and Harry.

I see the shadow of Luke's feet from the gap under the door. I sigh, starting to feel the guilt for yelling at him creep through the cracks of my mind. "Luke?"

"Yeah?" He calls back after a small pause.

"The Advil is in the kitchen, the cupboard above the stove." I suppose this could work. We'll just have to have a wall between us whenever we speak, so I won't ever have to meet his eyes again.

I listen for my bedroom door closing before I start to relax. I let the water soothe my tension as the soap soaks my skin in its fruity scent. All I can think is that I'm going to smell amazing and Jacob is not going to know what hit him.

After finishing off with my bath it doesn't take me more than half an hour to get ready. The whole time I still can't quite believe I'm going out with a guy I just met. And what luck too, that he happened to be free *tonight!*

I arrive at the restaurant early hoping to scope the place out and people watch for a bit before he arrives. Jacob had offered to pick me up on the way but I'm not that trusting. Even with the increased security in my apartment building you never know what can happen, especially with what happened to Gabby last year.

I'm just glad that there was a positive outcome for that whole situation. Plus, if our place hadn't been broken into she may not even be with Sam right now.

I'm led to a two-seater table off to the side covered with a white tablecloth and a red rose centrepiece. 'The Willow' isn't the fanciest restaurant in town but I suggested it because I know the chef, and he is A-M-A-Z-I-N-G. I suspect that even if the date goes as shit as it possibly could, at least the food will be good.

As soon as I sit down I feel the urge to pee. I knew I should have gone before I left the house, but I was in too much of a rush to get here early. Which, crazily enough, only just makes sense to me.

I try to distract myself from my bladder by looking around at the other customers. There's a few couples, a family at a large table near to the street facing window. It's still early for dinner, so I didn't really expect it to be busy. Hell, they only just started serving less than an hour ago. The waitress comes by to see if I need anything, and trying to look less pathetic I order myself a glass of white wine while I wait.

I'm surprised when only a few sips in I see Jacob as he walks across the street towards the restaurant. I push back my chair to stand as he enters but then think better of it. His eyes find me in the sparse room, and he smiles as he walks over.

"Hey." He sits down across from me eyeing the wine glass clasped in my hands. "Am I late? How long have you been here?"

"Not long. Sorry, I was early." I chuckle awkwardly.

"That's fine by me, I think I'll get myself started too." He flags down the waitress, orders a scotch and asks to see the menus.

"So what do you think you'll order?" Jacob asks as we both peruse the menu.

Honestly, I want the lasagna but being out on a date I feel under pressure to order something more sophisticated. Jacob is wearing a suit, a nice one too. I just feel he expects more from me than pasta. My eyes skim past that, my mouth clamping shut to keep the drool in. I paste on a fake ass smile as I find something else on the menu that I can stomach. "The mixed grain & roasted vegetable salad with salmon sounds nice."

I try my best not to gag at the sound of it. While I am a chef and I do like my food and trying new things, I also like sticking to the basics. I love burgers and fries and steak, and all those yummy things. I don't eat fancy shit just because I know how to make it.

"That does sound delicious. I think I might go with the barbecue glazed rump steak, gotta get in my protein." Is it just me or does that seem like an odd thing to say? Of course, I just ignore it and smile.

"Shall we order?" He asks as I slide my menu closed.

I agree and wave down the waitress. We place our orders but once the waitress leaves is when the date really begins.

"So, Tasha, what do you do?"

And here we go. "I'm a chef. What about you?"

"I'm a sports coach over at Martinsville High School."

"Oh, cool." That's definitely not what I was expecting. "So, you must really like kids, then? Or sports. Or both." I laugh at my own awkward little ramble.

"Yeah, I've always been interested in teaching. I love my job so it makes it that much easier going into work." I smile at the way his face lights up.

"That's great though, I love my job as well and I know what you mean. I really couldn't imagine doing anything else." Cooking is all I've ever really been good at, so I ran with it. I'm really lucky that it's gotten me this far.

We continue to chat on about our jobs, Jacob tells me about where he went to university and it flows nicely. I can even start to see us having a second date. Maybe.

A few minutes later Jacob excuses himself to wash up before our meals arrive. I down the rest of my wine before stopping the waitress and asking for a diet coke. I'm enjoying myself and the wine has definitely helped relax me but one's enough. Until later, when I get back home and finish off the bottle I've got waiting for me in the refrigerator.

Since Jacob has gone to the bathroom, I suppose I may as well seize the opportunity and go myself, I've been holding in that pee all throughout our conversation and at least a half hour beforehand.

I follow the sign to the toilets but what I find is far from what I expect. I pause in my footing and hide around the corner. At the end of the short corridor past the doors to the toilets, Jacob is pacing as he holds the phone to his ear. Shit. I've really gotta take a whiz but I don't want him to think I was following him. Or worse, eavesdropping on his conversation.

I finally decide that I have to head back to the table

and hold it until he returns. I promise I was about to leave but then I overhear the word 'babe' come from out of his mouth. *What?* It piques my interest, so I stay in place, hiding behind a fake plant and listen.

The more I hear the more furious I become. He's on the phone to another woman. His fuck buddy or his girlfriend I have no idea. There's a pause. He tells the person that he's got to get back to his business partner, tells them he 'loves them too' and that he can't wait to get back and punish her for being a filthy girl.

*Wow.* What a pig. I knew my first instincts about this guy were right. It's gone silent again. Oh, shit, I better move.

I run like hell back to the table and grab my purse before dashing out the door. I only slow down my run when I see my car in sight. I jump in and start the engine, I want to get as far away from here as possible. I want to go home, curl up in bed and completely forget that the dirt bag even exists.

I unlock the front door and push it open. Straight away I hear the TV playing and I know that someone, Luke, is home. Despite our run in earlier, I love that feeling. I love it even more knowing it's Luke that I'm coming home too. Except when I enter the living room he's not there, it's just Whiskey napping in her armchair.

"Luke?" I call out, turning the sound down on the telly. No sound follows. The apartment is dead. He must still be out. I guess that's for the best, I still don't know what to do or say when I see him next. Do I bring up the whole flash dance? Will I be able to look him in the eye? Holy shit, will he be able to look me in the eye? That definitely had to be the worst-case scenario, right?

Maybe I should pull a F.R.I.E.N.D.S episode and try to catch him out. But we've already got sexual tension, would it really be wise to add an everlasting naked image of Luke to the mix. Probably not.

# CHAPTER SEVEN
*Luke*

"Luke, my man." One of my oldest friends, Jake, drunkenly shouts out from across the bar. It draws a few stares but thankfully, the bar is still pretty quiet. "Where have you been lately? We've missed you around these parts of town."

I laugh at Jake's dramatic antics as he stumbles away from the pack. "I was here just a few weeks ago, you moron."

"Lukey, my man." Wow, okay, he's had more to drink than usual. The match isn't even at half time, how long have they been here. My guess is the majority of the day.

Meeting up at the local sports bar has been a tradition since before we were even legal. And, right now, catching up with my boys is just the distraction from a certain brunette that I need.

I couldn't stand being in the same enclosing space as Natasha for any longer. To know that she was only in the next room over, naked and primping herself out for a date with someone else. Her rocking body had taken up a permanent residence in my brain the second I laid eyes on it. I ran. As fast as I could, my cock still as hard as diamonds, I rushed somewhere I knew I would be safe from my temptress of a roommate.

I cut across to join the guys at one of the high tables dotted around the room. It's still fairly early so most of the patrons are just here for the football. Later on, the match will end and the place will fill with young singletons like myself looking for any place that serves liquor.

Maybe that's what I need, a hook-up. Some loose casual fun. It's been so long since the last time I got some action. Trying to recall, the last time was probably Nicola, the chick that helplessly followed me around Europe. The only reason I couldn't complain at the time was because I was hitting that on a regular basis, whenever and wherever I needed.

A cold shiver runs down the length of my spine at even just the thought of that woman.

I spot a blonde standing at the very end of the bar. She's cute. Normally she'd be just my type. I'd say she's about average height but between her short dress and her high heels her legs look long and toned. Her tight sequined dress leaves very little to the imagination.

She's with another chick but her eyes are on me. I see her friend talking away but I've already captured the blonde's attention, there's no way she could be hearing a word her friend is saying. With my back against the table, I do another quick survey of the crowd before turning back to my friends.

I'll have to keep blondie in mind for later. She could very well be what I need right now. Quick, easy and fun. No strings attached fun. That's what I liked, that's who I am. Although I love my nephew and I can see the major love between my sister and Adam, I've never wanted that sort of relationship. But, I also think, a love like that - that lasts, can't be forced or found with just anyone. I think you get one shot at that kind of love. The unconditional, withstand anything love.

If I did ever find that one special person, my soul-mate, then I'd like to believe that I'd be open to it. The whole shebang, marriage, kids, settling down and sharing my life with someone. But until that person comes along, I'm happy by myself.

As the night progresses, I try my best to keep a side

eye on the blonde. I notice she gets approached twice by guys, who are probably looking for the same thing I am, but they both get turned away. I'm hoping I'll have better luck later.

When the football game ends, everyone's on a high at the big win. The T.V. commentary gets turned down and the music gets turned up. I look around to see the bar far more crowded than before, I even spot a hen do taking up residence in a corner booth. I take a drag of my fifth beer, the cool liquid sliding smoothly down the back of my throat. It's not long after that I notice movement from the corner of my eye.

I watch as the blonde pushes away from the bar, she makes her way toward my corner of the bar. At first, I think she might be approaching me, but then she sashays on past. I would've thought she'd ignored me completely but the dramatic wink she tosses out in my direction speaks volumes.

I think over my next move. This is it, the time for my big play. I could follow her, accidentally bump into her, introduce myself that way. I can't imagine what good will come from following her but I do it anyway. She could freak out that a creep followed her to the bathrooms. Or, maybe I could casually bump into her and introduce myself. Hell, it's worked before. Instead, I decide I'll wait until she gets back to the bar and then send a drink her way, a Cosmo - what she's been sipping away at all night.

As the bartender slides the drink in front of her, I watch as her face scrunches up in confusion. The guy points over to me, I raise my glass and wink. By this time, what's left of my friend group has dispersed to drunkenly grind up against their latest catch. I finish off my beer and pull out my phone to check the time, nearly eight o'clock. There's a text from Gabby and immediately my mind wanders to Natasha.

**Tash had a shit night, could you please be extra sweet to her tonight? - Gabby**

*Mmm.* Speaking of the irresistible angel. I start to worry myself over her date. Had it really gone that badly? Was she okay? At least I know she's at home and not out with some idiot that clearly doesn't know how to take care of such a precious package.

My train of thought makes me flag down the nearest bartender. "Three shots of tequila."

I down my first two shots, reaching for the third I'm not quick enough. Slim fingers ending in long bright pink nails wrap around the small glass.

I turn to face my thief, the blonde that I've been eyeing all night. She's even hotter up close. Maybe a little too much makeup. That's one thing I'll never be able to wrap my mind around if you're already naturally pretty then why try to cover that up?

"I'm Kandice." Her voice is low and sultry, just the sound makes my dick stir to life.

"Luke." Her glossy pink smile widens. "It's nice to meet you, Kandice."

She brings the shot glass up to her lips and throws her head back, downing the burning liquid.

"Would you like another?" I ask. I'm a little rusty but I'm trying my hardest to summon some charm from deep down - the old Luke. He had charm in bucket loads.

"Not yet. Maybe after a dance?" She bats her lashes up at me and holds her hand out, awaiting mine. As much as I hate dancing, I'd hate to turn her down even more.

I place my hand on top of hers, she drags me away from the cluster of tables and towards the mass of moving and swaying bodies.

I actually don't mind the song that's playing, so I sway on the spot. Her arms wrap around my neck, pushing her body into mine. Soon, the song changes into something faster, and a little more provocative. I feel her lips brush against my neck and her hips move a little more daringly. And while her lips feel nice, all I can seem to worry about is how she's probably getting her lip gloss all over my neck.

In an effort to focus my mind on the beautiful blonde that's wrapping herself around me like a burrito, I move my hips faster. Harder. Grinding myself against her as she rides my thigh.

Her lips move up over my jaw, kissing the corner of my lips. When she leans in further, pressing her slick lips fully against mine, I push back with just as much enthusiasm. Her nails dig into my shoulders and a groan reverberates up her throat.

Managing to pull ourselves apart we down some more shots at the bar before continuing to make out in the middle of the dancefloor. The time passes by smoothly now. The bar is at full capacity and I've now completely lost track of all my friends. I'm at a state of numbness that I'm comfortable with. The liquor has softened my brain; all my thoughts are soft and the colour yellow.

Kandice's' kisses turn more fevered and I have a distinct feeling she's getting impatient for more. She pulls away and giggles to herself. I watch as she unwraps herself from me and steps back. It's not light enough to see, but I'm pretty sure I can feel a pool of her wetness on my jean-clad thigh.

I only wish I was that turned on. I may have been

supporting a semi most of our time dancing, but unfortunately nothing more than that. For some reason, the hands that are roaming my body aren't turning me on. Maybe it's the alcohol taking effect. Maybe it's because my hands are wanting the feel of soft curves where there are none. Maybe because my mind pictures the petite brunette that now takes up residence in the bedroom next to mine. I know it's the hands touching me that are the problem, they don't belong to the right person.

Suddenly Kandice grips my hand and leads me towards the restrooms. I let her lead me because I need this. I want to feel like my normal self again She pushes heavily against the side exit door and steps out into the back alley. If I were in the right frame of mind I'd turn us around and send her home. She's very clearly drunk and I'd be taking advantage of her. But, as I am in a similar state of inebriation I continue on my quest to get into her pants. Or under her skirt, as it were.

She pushes against my shoulders, shoving me back against rough bricks. Her lips clash against mine and I notice the lack of gloss. Her hand travels from my shoulder down to my chest, feeling over my ridged abs to the belt of my jeans. Her fingers brush against me, working my cock over the material of my jeans. She cups and strokes my semi while I close my eyes tight

shut. I try my hardest to just give in, to feel the pleasure of her touch.

When nothing happens, I pull away from the
sloppy tongue dance we were doing. I admit defeat.

"I can't, I'm sorry."

"Is something wrong?" She looks pointedly down
at my crotch as if expecting my dick to answer her.

"Yeah. I don't mean this the way it's going to sound
but, it's not me, it's you." Before I even have half a
second to explain a sound resonates around us and my
cheek blooms with heat.

Fair enough, I definitely deserved that one.

"What a jerk! What a waste of a night." She's
already walking away, exiting the alleyway out onto the
street.

I wait a few minutes trying to pull myself together
enough to figure out what the fuck just happened.
When nothing comes to mind but Natasha I know I
need to get out of here.

# CHAPTER EIGHT

"Oh fuck," I grunt out loud. I grip my shaft tighter in my palm trying to imagine what it would feel like if I were inside tiny little Natasha.

I close my eyes to picture her. I'm not having much luck; I've been trying to get off for fifteen minutes. It's just not happening.

I hear footsteps down the hallway but I can't tell if they're in my imagination or real life. I find out when there's an audible gasp from across the room. I open my eyes to see my Natasha standing in the doorway. *Hmm, I guess I'm not the only one who barges in without knocking.*

"I thought I heard," her mouth stops moving as her

eyes lock on my bare cock in my hand. "Something," she weakly finishes her sentence.

Her eyes don't leave my hand as it continues to stroke my dick. I keep moving, watching her watch me is maybe the most erotic thing I've ever seen. She doesn't have to do anything, with her just standing and staring I can already start to feel my balls tightening.

My hips start thrusting up from the bed to meet my hand. I can imagine I'm fucking her, her tight pussy clenching me as she edges closer and closer towards her orgasm. She'd be wearing the exact expression that she has on now, that cute blush that tries to cover the intrigue and lust that fires in her eyes. She wants it. I know she wants it and I bet if I were to touch her right now her pussy would be dripping wet.

All that wetness just for me. It has me salivating for a taste of her rosy hidden flesh.

My body almost convulses as everything comes surging to the forefront. My orgasm rushes over me and my seed squirts out onto my belly. I slow down my hand, milking my cock for the last of my cum. I look back up to see Natasha chewing on her lip.

Our eyes connect and something passes between us. The feeling lingers causing goose bumps to rise on my exposed skin. Never have I had such an intimate moment with someone, feeling so exposed but so fucking hot at the same time.

One second she's there and the next she's gone. She flies out of the room leaving me alone as I recover from, what's definitely a top ten orgasm. And now she's going to freak out and continue freezing me out like she's been doing for the past week. In the short space of time I've been here I've learned one thing for sure, Natasha is skittish. She puts on a solid brave face until you start to get close - only then you can see the fractures. She keeps everyone at arm's length because then it's easier to hide what you're really feeling.

I think she's been hiding from me because I can see past it all. I see past all the fluff to the tender goddess that's hiding within. Sometimes I wonder if she sees it if she even knows that she doesn't show off her full self to anyone outside of her comfort zone. I'll be forever grateful that I forced my way into her apartment and therefore into her comfort zone.

I can't contain my evil ass laugh as I jump in the shower. *Boy, am I going to regret that later*.

And I prove myself right not even half an hour later. I'm sitting at the breakfast bar when Tash finally storms out of her room, right past me and then slams the front door closed behind her. Well, that confirms it, she's totally pissed. I knew it.

Ever since I walked in on her in the bath she's been hiding. I've been patient with her, I've given her space. I don't know what else to do. And, it's driving me nuts because I can't get the image of her naked, wet, curvy little body out of my head. But then her walking in on me wanking off... I'm guessing that's pushed her into the valley of pissed off even more.

I'm mad at myself for letting her see that but I also can't get the image of her chewing her lip out of my head. The look in her eyes was like fire, the way it flared and danced. It was truly hypnotising.

She's so fucking sexy, and she doesn't even know the effect she has. The things I'd do to that lithe little body if I had the chance. She's so tiny though, I'd be afraid of breaking her in two. But the things she makes me feel without even touching me is incredible and so powerful. Maybe I'd be the one to break in two if she had her way with me.

It's my day off from work but I'm not really sure what to do with myself. I had planned to spend the day trying to fix things with Tash and working to make our things a bit less awkward after the whole bathroom incident. Things haven't been the same since then. She's been avoiding me like crazy and I hate it. Now, she's going to be even more standoffish.

I'm now left with my last resort to get her to talk to

me. I tried giving her space, that only ended up doubling my frustrations. I've tried giving her time, and that's ended with her walking in on me jerking out my frustrations. After which she'll probably never look me in the eye again. No, I'll need help, in fact, this is a job for a professional.

I can't help pacing as the phone rings against my ear. *Come on Gabby, pick up.*

"Gabby! Finally, what took so long?" I huff.

"Well, Sam wa-" She doesn't get any more than that out before I quickly cut her off.

"I *really* don't wanna know what Sam was doing. Look, I need your help." The only issue, what do I say happened. If I say anything too detailed she'll start asking questions, or start placing blame. No, I just need to keep it as vague as possible. "Tash has been avoiding me."

"Why?" Hmm. Why indeed Gabby. I suck my lips between my teeth to contain the truth of why Tash isn't talking to me. I could laugh at how ridiculous this all is but I'm pretty sure Gabby is going to kill me when she finds out the real reason behind Natasha's resistance. It's a pretty valid reason not to talk to someone but Gabby's going to be even more pissed when she realises I used her to get Natasha's attention.

"I really can't think of any reason?" I throw my

voice to sound as innocent as possible like I'm the victim in all of this. "I don't know what else I can do. Could you please talk to her? Just tell me how to fix it. I'm begging you, Gabs."

"Yeah yeah, no problem. Get your panties out of a twist," she sasses.

"Thank you." I heave a relieved sigh before we hang up. I should have just went straight to her for advice last week. My chest feels a little lighter knowing that Gabby will sort it out or at least try. I know Gabby, and while she'll be pissed, she's also rooting for Natasha and I to get together. She'll do anything to get me back into Tash's good graces.

# CHAPTER NINE

I can't ignore the guilt that's eating away at my gut. In my insistence to avoid Luke, I've been finding all new ways and reasons to get out of the house. At midnight last night, I even signed up for an art class. I've taken swimming lessons, picked up extra shifts at work, I've volunteered to walk a friend from works' dogs. I don't even like dogs!

But while I've been busy and keeping out of the house, I've been having to leave Whiskey all by her lonesome. Well, I know Luke is there sometimes but that's not the point. I can already see the change in her. She's had a chip on her shoulder since I decided to go out and get a life. I think she must think I'm neglecting her. I didn't even have a chance to say goodbye to her this morning.

I had been in such a hurry to storm out leaving Luke staring at my dust that I'd not only forgotten about my cat but also my swimming costume and my uniform for work.

My phone rings, again. And yet again, it's Gabby. This must be the fourth or fifth time she's rang this morning. I'm starting to think something might be wrong but I don't feel ready to talk to her, not yet. We haven't really had the chance to talk much lately and I think she's starting to notice that I'm avoiding her too. I suck in a breath, pull up my big girl panties and answer the phone to my best friend.

"Well, heeeeeey Gabby." I sing out cheerily, not wanting to tip her off.

"Don't you 'hey Gabby' me, little miss. Where the hell have you been? I've been calling and calling, and I know something's up when you're not picking up your phone. Now, spill it!"

"Nothing's up, I've just been...busy?" Wow, I really am a terrible liar. Even I heard the questioning tone in my voice there, that was pathetic. I may have been going overboard with the errands and classes this week but anyone who knows me, knows I'm usually never busy. It even feels weird saying it.

"Liar. Tell me what's going on with you," she begs.

"Luke walked in on me naked." Although it's kind of yesterday's news now.

"What!"

"Yeah. And then I walked in on him jerking off." And it was fucking *H-O-T*.

"WHAT!"

"Holy motherfucking shit. When? Oh, my god, that's why he called to ask if I'd check up on you. He sounded funny on the phone but I didn't stop to think that something might've actually happened between you guys."

"You mean you've spoken to Luke? But he didn't tell you? Gabby, it only happened this morning."

"No, he's much better at hiding things from me than you are. You're so easy to read." True, which is exactly why I've been hiding outside where no one can find me.

"I'm so embarrassed, Gabby. I don't know what to do."

"Okay, so calm yourself. You've been naked in front of plenty of people before, why is it different this time? Hell, I've walked in on you naked so many times you'd think I was waiting outside your door 24/7 for you to strip. You've never been embarrassed in front of me."

Well, yeah but it's not the same. We both have all the same bits, as immature as that sounds. "You're a girl?"

It's more of a guess than a solid answer to her question. The truth is I don't know the reason behind my uncomfortableness. Maybe it's because Luke is a gorgeous reincarnation of a Greek god and I'm... well, I'm certainly not a goddess. It's all round intimidating.

"Yeah, that's not it. Try again."

"Honestly, I don't know. I just know that I feel uncomfortable in my body whenever Luke is around."

"Oh, yep. Now we're getting somewhere." Her voice alone scares me, it's her conspiring voice.

"No-no, don't you dare. You're not allowed to do that voice with me. Don't think I don't know that tone." I sass right back to Gabby.

"Has someone got a little crush, Tash?"

"Pfft." Fuck, what'd I do that for? 'Pfft' is like the universal sign for 'what I'm about to say is bullshit'. "What I mean is, no someone has not. There's no crushes in this house. There's no crushes in sight. Everything is strictly crush free."

"Okay, if you say so." Phew. "So have you just skipped straight to like-liking him?" She bursts into a fit of giggles and I swear I've never been so close to hanging up on her in my life.

"I'm going to go now."

"No, wait. What do you want me to say to Luke when he rings me back later?"

"Tell him to go to hell, on my behalf of course."

"Um, no I'd rather not."

"Fine, tell him to grow a pair of balls and come talk to me himself, unless he's afraid I'll bite them off."

"Hmph, yeah I'm not going to say that either. Hey! How was his dick? I've always been curious." I frown not liking the thought of anyone else thinking so intimately about Luke.

"GABBY!" I whisper shout, not wanting to draw any attention to the conversation I'm a part of right now. I'm in a public park for Christ's sake.

"What? You can't blame a girl for being curious. Your lack of answer, by the way, says loads. Either it was microscopic and not worth mentioning or it was massive, like too big to fit in this conversation M-A-S-S-I-V-E."

"Oh my god. I can't even," I hate that I'm laughing at her when she's being a lil' bitch but that's just Gabby being Gabby.

"I knew you'd fall for him, just like I knew he'd fall for you. I'll let Luke know that you're thinking about his balls. Talk soon, okay?"

"Gabb-" And she hung up. That stone-cold bitch.

Wait, did she say Luke was falling for me? Ugh, I don't have time for this right now. Looking at my watch I decide I'll have to postpone this freak out until later. I exit the park and make my way to work.

I read somewhere that sunshine helped to improve moods. So as soon as I caught sight of today's rays I thought I'd give it a shot. I've been sitting in the park for just over two hours soaking up the last of today's sunshine. I was only reading but I had already started to feel myself relaxing. Until Gabby rang that is.

Having an extra uniform in my locker saves me from making the trek all the way home before I start my shift at the restaurant. I throw it on, wave hello to some of my co-workers, the ones I actually like, and then prepare myself for a long ass shift.

The shift is broken up nicely when my manager comes into the kitchen an hour later asking me into her office. Stevie isn't the easiest person to get along with. If she likes you, you're blessed. If she doesn't, you're screwed, and she'll let you know it. Me, she seems to like, well, my cooking anyway.

Her office is more or less next door to the kitchen as she likes to keep a close eye on everything. I follow behind her into the small room. It feels wrong calling it an office, it's more like a small landfill site. There're files and papers everywhere, the bin is overflowing with garbage and I'm pretty sure... yep, that's a half-eaten sandwich on her desk. I recenter myself and try not to judge, I know how hard Stevie works - so what if she's not the cleanest person.

"These were dropped off for you earlier." She plonks herself into her desk chair and points towards the bunch of red and white roses that are taking place on a side table.

"Thanks...?" My curiosity gets the better of me. I move closer and pick up the small note that's sticking out. Clear as day it has my name printed on the front.

Who would send me flowers? I'm pretty sure no one has ever sent me flowers. I don't even know what I've done to deserve flowers. Maybe they're for a different Natasha. I'd still keep them, they're far too pretty to give back to their actual *intended* owner.

In the weirdest of ways, I'm not even surprised that the note is signed from Luke. He's so sweet and charming, and probably the only guy on the planet to still send a girl flowers. I mean, we girls like diamonds but flowers are a close second, especially roses.

'I've missed you. Please forgive me. - Luke'

It's a little bit suspicious that I get these only a couple of hours after talking to Gabby about the man in question. Maybe I should just get over myself and quit ignoring him. The truth is, despite the naked spectacle and the jerking incident, I've missed him too.

And I can't deny that maybe Gabby's words have gotten to me. Luke's very impressive dick aside, I do really like him. Plus, who am I to deny his too-big-for-this-conversation dick?

"TASH?" I hear Luke call out as soon as I swing open the apartment door. It's late and I hadn't expected him to still be up.

Great! What I had planned for tomorrow can now happen tonight. My whole shift I couldn't stop thinking about him and all the different ways this could go. All the scenarios played on repeat in my head. At one point, I thought of just going up to him and kissing him. Then I blushed and continued my job with my head down hoping no one would see the dirty thoughts plaguing my mind.

I drop my keys on the side table and my coat on the hook. The apartment is warm and smells amazing.

I wander around the corner into the kitchen where Luke is cooking up, what looks to be, chicken stir-fry. He sets the wok back on the stove and turns around handing me a glass of white wine. It's all too much. I almost feel like I'm going to burst into tears at any moment. I rush forward to wrap my arms around Luke's torso. "I'm so sorry," I whisper as I bury my head into his chest.

We stand there for a minute and Luke just holds me. It's the hug I've needed and longed for all damn day.

After a while, Luke pulls back holding me at arm's length. "You have nothing to apologise for. I'm the one that's sorry."

"But you have nothing to be sorry for, it's me that's been acting silly," I shake my head and argue.

"I'm sorry that I've been acting so weird around you. And despite how much it rocked my world, I'm sorry you had to see such an intimate thing. I only rang Gabby because I knew you probably wouldn't have talked to me ever again after this morning. You wouldn't even let me apologize for walking in on you in the bathroom. But Natasha, you have to know how badly I want you. I haven't been able to stop picturing you naked."

This would be the scene in the movies where I would sharply inhale and then it would cut to the end. And I'm not just talking about Twilight - loads of movies do that. But instead, my mind feels numb and overwhelmed. So, I let my body react instead, by reaching up and pressing my lips against his.

Neither one of us move until finally, I realise my mistake and pull away. "I'm so sorry. Again."

"It's fine. Just in shock that's all."

"Luke, I don't want things to be awkward between us - despite me just kissing you. I just want things to go back to normal."

"Okay." His mouth may be saying okay but his eyes are telling a different story altogether. They're saying 'for now'. "How about you sit down and chill out, I've made us some dinner."

I nod along and do what he says. It's been a very long day and I don't think I've got any fight left in me. But I can't help smiling knowing that everything is back to being okay between Luke and I. I don't know what will happen in the future but for now, I'm just happy to have my friend slash roommate back.

# CHAPTER TEN

*Luke*

It's fucking cold. I know it's only March, here in Aurora that usually means cold. But, the last few days have been sunny. I had begun to think that the weather was on the rise. Maybe not.

I walk through the door of the apartment and thank the lord that Natasha has the fire on. The apartment has central heating so the electric fire that sits below the mantle is more decorative than anything else. But tonight, I feel warmer from just looking at it. It also means that Natasha is home and after all that's happened, I'd like to spend some more time with her. Even if it's just as friends and I'm horny the entire time, I'll take whatever I can get right now. And, the thought of 'friendly' snuggling into Natasha sounds irresistible right now.

"Natasha?" I call out, dropping my bag and coat at the door. I flop onto the couch ready to relax after a long day at work.

"Yeah, in here." After a few seconds, she reappears from around the corner. A smile takes over my face when I take in her appearance.

"I thought you had work tonight?" I smirk and pointedly raise my eyebrow at her penguin print pyjama pants. She has her hair up in a messy bun, a baggy sweatshirt covering her torso and fuzzy socks on her feet.

She fakes a half-assed cough, "I'm sick."

"No, you're Pinocchio," I laugh and rise from my position on the couch. Although her outfit is insanely adorable, it also looks really comfy and reminds me that I should change.

Her hand on my arm stops me as I move past her. "I was just going to put a movie on, you can join if you like?"

Mmm. "Depends which movie?" I'm full of shit, the movie could literally-fucking-be Pinocchio and I wouldn't give a damn. There is nothing that she can put on that I wouldn't want to watch with her.

"Ghostbusters?"

"Okay, just let me change first." She continues about, setting her pillows and blankets up on the floor. I quickly rush down the hall trying to escape the mental image of fucking her on her living room floor.

The raging hard on makes it uncomfortable to change clothes but I manage it. I throw on my track pants and a clean shirt to be modest. Even on the cold nights, my pyjamas consist of boxer shorts and that's it. But for Natasha's sake, I cover up especially since she's insisting things go back to normal. She doesn't realise yet that we're so far past normal that I can't even see it from where we are now.

I'm strolling into the lounge room to re-join Natasha when a sound startles me. Immediately I dive for Natasha, and we fall to the floor. A loose strand of hair falls over her forehead and tangles against her eyelashes. My heart beats wildly in my chest as I hold her tightly. Slowly lifting my hand, I slip the strand free and tuck it behind her ear. The movement, ever so innocent, feels like the most intimate thing I've ever done with a woman.

"I think it was just from outside..." Tash whispers.

Our eyes are locked and I've almost forgotten about the resounding bang. "Oh, yeah. We should probably check it out."

I slowly lift off of her. In any normal situation, I

would probably feel some hint of embarrassment but all that's burning inside of me is the desire to be inside of her.

We shake ourselves off before moving towards the window overlooking the street. My eyes sweep up and down but nothing looks out of place. Maybe a few more people out on the street than normal.

"Oh, shit," she gasps.

"What? What is it?" I scan wildly for what the hell she could be looking at.

"The Ollivander Building." With her words, my eyes swing down to the very end of the street. The Ollivander is an old apartment building a few blocks down.

"Fuck," I can't help my surprise at the building alight with flames. The windows on the fifth floor are shattered and I highly suspect that was what the noise was.

I squint to see a fire engine on the other side of the building, and it looks like the police have just pulled up. We watch in horror as they evacuate the building surrounding the fire. More cops arrive to calm down the panic from the crowds.

A knock of the apartment door has Natasha jumping out of her skin. "I'll get it," I whisper still not being able to tear my eyes from the blaze.

I tear the door open to find the apartment manager.

I haven't met him before but Natasha has pointed him out a time or two. "Hey."

"I'm going around warning all the tenants that the police have asked for everyone to stay indoors. The fire won't, in any way, affect us, and they're trying to keep the streets clear for emergency services only. As soon as they clear out, you'll be able to resume your normal activities." He nods curtly before moving on to knock on Mrs. Adelman's door.

I roll my eyes at the slimy weasel. I bet he would've hung around longer if it were Natasha that had answered the door. Even the notion makes me growl with annoyance.

"What's wrong? Who was it?" Natasha asks with her back turned, still pressing up against the living room window.

"Apparently, the cops have requested that we stay indoors for the time being. To keep the streets clear." My voice twiddles down as I catch sight of the flashing lights from outside. I'm across the room but I'm suddenly very distracted by the sight of her. I find myself very aware of her movements. Her arms wrap around her waist as she draws her body in, making her seem even tinier. I'm curious to know if she actually realises she's doing it, is she cold? Is she scared?

I hear another reverberating blast. It's so loud. I

wince, not only from the shock but also because it means the fire is still going. The longer it blazes, the more people are likely to get hurt, or worse.

Natasha visibly shivers. I can sense her fear from across the room. She turns away from the road. I try to catch her eye, but she's spellbound. I want to help her but I don't know what to do. I take a couple of steps closer. She's shaken by the horrible events playing out down the street, and the universe is practically screaming for me to take her in my arms and hold her. I watch her, waiting...

When her eyes flicker up to meet mine, decision made. I walk forward to comfort her the best I can.

# CHAPTER ELEVEN

I watch, frozen, as Luke crosses the room. His strong arms wrap around my body and pull me into him, enclosing me in his body heat. It's so nice being in his arms that I snuggle in even further, wanting to be as close as physically able.

His hands run soothingly up and down my back. The movement giving me comfort, but then his hand slips, landing a bit lower than it should. My breathing stops as I wait for his hand to move again. Will he retreat? Or is he finally going to give me what I need? That luscious thick rod that he hides, just barely, underneath his jeans.

Luke's grip on me tightens, pulling me incredibly closer. Our bodies are crushed together and then, just like that, the air around us changes. It sparks something anew, something exciting and tingly.

"Luke?" My voice sounds foreign to my own ears, it's disoriented and gravelly. I stare a hole into his chest afraid to look up and meet his eyes. I can already feel the weight of his lusting stare, to see it would probably light fire to my insides.

"Natasha." His breath whispers against my neck, causing goose pimples to rise across my skin. I'm still not used to it but I love that he is the only one, besides my parents, that call me by my full name. It just makes our friendship mean that little bit extra. Well, to me it does anyway.

His lips are only a hair width away from my neck. I can feel their heat but it's not enough. I tilt myself just that tiny bit closer to meet his lips, to spark that first touch. When his lips press against my neck, it's not just a kiss, he immediately latches on. If my eyes hadn't already rolled into the back of my head I would've been worrying that he'd never let me go.

His lips make their way up and down the side of my exposed neck, sucking and nipping along the sensitive skin there.

"...Luke." I hear myself moan and it startles me out of my daze. "Luke, maybe we shouldn't...?"

That certainly gets his attention. He pulls back,

looking me in the eye and then deadly serious says, "Maybe we should."

His certainty buzzes through me. He really wants this, and he's willing to throw everything else out the window to have it. I see his lips start to descend, slowly, giving me more than enough time to back out. Making a split-second decision I reach up on my tiptoes to meet his lips.

The kiss isn't fireworks and rainbows, that shit's not real, but it's sure as hell close enough for me. I've never felt anything so strong in my life, except maybe Luke's biceps. They're hard as fuck. But this kiss is intense and it only gets hotter by the second. His tongue is quick to sweep into my mouth and take over the show. We're trapped in time in this lip lock until his hand that's low on my back starts to creep even lower.

Then his hand isn't on my back anymore but instead, grabbing at my ass. His touch provokes my hands to wander. Dragging themselves up and over his sculpted shoulders and digging my nails into his muscled skin.

I tug against the material of Luke's shirt wanting it gone. I need more of his skin. He gets the idea and quickly pulls his shirt off over his head. And it's the first time I really get to stand there and inspect him, inch by inch, muscle by muscle. I've seen him naked before but this time I'm allowed to drool. This time I'm looking at more than just his cock, I get to take my time going over every muscled ridge of his entire body.

Luke's lips move down my neck, my head lolls to the side. When he comes to the edge of my sweatshirt his hands slip underneath it pushing it up until he tears it over my head. I'm not wearing a bra and while the sudden unveiling leaves me feeling a shiver, I'm glad to have one less obstacle in our way.

Luke continues his blazing trail of kisses down my chest. I'm shocked when he suddenly pulls back. "What's wrong?"

He grunts as he looks around. I see it on his face when he finally finds what he's looking for. Then I'm being lifted into the air onto the couch. I'm now standing a foot or so above him. As his mouth latches on to my nipple, I get the reasoning behind my relocation. His hands run smoothly up and down my thighs as his tongue weaves different patterns around my nipples.

When his teeth gently nip me, my knees buckle but Luke's hands keep me from falling. He releases my left nipple to go in search for my right. I wrap my arms around his head, trapping him there - hoping he never moves. Lifting my leg up to wrap around his torso, I need to be closer to him. For our bodies to touch and connect more than they are now. Luke grips my leg and tries to coax the other one up with his hand.

Both of my legs wrap tightly around Luke's waist as I slide down his body into his awaiting arms. I can't pull my eyes away from his as he lays me down on the blanketed floor. The intensity coursing through his irises sends a warmth running through my veins.

Luke pulls off his pants before hastily wiggling me out of my pyjamas and my underwear. I feel his erection, hard and hot as he presses his lower half against mine. With his face hovering over mine, just out of reach, I push myself up to close the distance between our lips.

The kiss is passionate but fast, there's a sense of urgency that I've never felt before - I'm pretty sure it's coming from me. His chest rubs against mine and the slight touch causes my nipples to harden painfully, screaming for attention. He does it again, slower this time and I groan at the friction. His every movement is controlled but filled with the need for more.

Our bodies line up perfectly despite Luke being so much taller than me. There's no clothing left between us, nothing stopping me from lifting my hips and offering myself up to him.

His body starts to move down my body, his lips

leaving sweet kisses in their wake. I shudder as his teeth bite into the soft flesh just above my hip.

He nudges open my knees exposing my bare flesh. My first instinct is to cower and cover myself. The first time being this vulnerable with someone is always an internal struggle. But one look at Luke and I feel secure. *And scared.* The two are complete opposites and to feel both at the same time, it's all very wishy-washy.

There's so much emotion on his face and that's what scares me. I know that this means as much to him as it does to me. This can't just be a one night stand, there's no way I can have my fill of Luke in just one sitting. A small sense of dread settles in my gut as I think about what will happen after, tomorrow maybe? I don't want to think about it. So, I push my internal struggles aside and force myself to just stay in the present.

When Luke finally settles himself between my thighs he pauses and hovers for a second. I tilt my hips slightly and that seems to surge him on. He takes one long lick, from my entrance up to my clit. Already I can feel my chest heaving as I try to catch my breath.

It's been awhile since anyone has touched me there. Or anywhere. As much as I want Luke to go to town on my clit I want him inside me more. I'm embarrassingly needy for him, so much so that this feels unnecessary.

"Luke," I didn't intend on begging but I will if I have to, I need more. I'm desperate for it. I squeeze his bare shoulder to get his attention.

His tongue circles my clit, the little bundle of nerves throbbing already. His eyes flicker up to meet mine. And it's the most erotic thing I've seen, to have all of his attention so focused on me makes me feel like I'm the only woman in the world. "Please."

Luke's mouth unlatches from me giving me only an ounce of relief, but instead of moving back up my body he sits up, kneeling on his knees. His hands grip my hips lifting me, so I'm off the floor, my legs spread and resting over his open thighs. He aligns himself to my entrance, my breath hitches in anticipation. His tip glides through my folds, taking the same up and down route that his tongue did just moments ago. He pauses at my opening once again, nudging forward slightly, almost as if testing the waters.

Luke's grip on my hips tightens, holding me in place as he thrusts forward. The sharp movement causes my legs to fall open even further, killing any distance between us. Luke pulls all the way out, and suddenly it's like there's an empty cave inside of me. I can feel it, the emptiness, in a way I've never felt it before. I need him back; I need him to fill the space. He moves inside of me and I lift my hips trying to match his rhythm the best I can.

Luke grunts, his thrusts becoming more frantic as we both edge closer and closer to what I assume will be the most addicting high I'll ever feel. My heart beats faster and faster inside my chest as the pleasure I've been searching for finally explodes within my body. I grasp at the tingling sensation of my orgasm as I watch Luke come undone. His body shakes violently before he caves. He holds most of his body weight off of me but he's now close enough that I can feel his radiating heat. His lips press a quick peck to my lips before they continue down my neck. Tender kisses cover every inch of my neck and face, unlike before these kisses are gentle - almost innocent. And they're probably my favourite.

As Luke rolls over I have to chew on my lip to keep my disappointment bottled. I like feeling close to him, especially since I don't know how long this is going to last. I see Luke's chest heave up and down, and I know he's just as worn out as I am.

I try to calm my breathing and to calm my mind as Luke drifts off to sleep. He looks so sweet and carefree with his eye closed, his hair tousled carelessly. The blanket barely covers the both of us but it's thinness allows me to see every bump and curve he's got.

*Ohmyfuckinggod.* What have I done!

Yep, that sounds about right. Once my brain has had a chance to catch up that's when it really starts to sink in. I can't do this. I don't know what Luke wants, or expects. From what I've heard about him he doesn't like to go around the same merry-go-round twice. Was that what this was? I don't know and I could really just slap myself silly for not asking first.

That's what usually happens, we girls ask 'what are we doing?', that kills the mood but then, at least you know what you're doing. I didn't ask, I jumped right to it. I think maybe deep down I didn't wanna know. I didn't wanna be told that we were just fooling around. With anyone else that response might not have bothered me so much but this is Luke. And I like Luke way too much to be able to handle any response that isn't 'I like you Natasha'.

I can't do casual sex, not with Luke. What if that's what he thinks this is? *What the hell was I thinking?*

Hmm... I was thinking that Luke's nice, and smart, and funny. And hot as hell. Looking over at his still form I can almost imagine the steam rising from his body because he's that hot.

"Shh," Luke's arm flings across my stomach, pulling me in closer to his side. "Go back to sleep."

I don't know how but it was like he felt my panic. I made no sound, no move but yet he just knew. That sounds crazy, there's probably some explanation but I like the thought of him being able to read me so easily. Despite the fact that I have no control over this situation and that I have no idea what's going to happen tomorrow, I let myself sink into Luke's embrace.

Everything will work out. And if it doesn't, I'm moving in with Gabby.

# CHAPTER TWELVE

Luke

I wasn't asleep long last night before I felt Natasha tense up next to me. I don't know what it was for sure, that was causing her to worry but I'm guessing it wasn't a bad dream.

I wake up early, not on purpose but I'm glad it works out that way. After throwing on my pants, I tiptoe around the kitchen in the hopes that I won't wake up Natasha.

I pull out the frying pan to make bacon and eggs. When I notice that Natasha is starting to stir from sleep I flick the coffee machine on. Breakfast is nearly ready so I'm hoping the smell of coffee will lure her into the kitchen.

"You made breakfast? Again?" Natasha stands in

the doorway rubbing the sleep from her face. "You better be careful; a girl could get used to this sort of treatment."

"Good morning sunshine!" I finish plating up her food and set it in front of her.

"Could I have the mustard, please?" She doesn't even have to finish her question because I'm already placing the bottle in front of her. I smile and sneak a quick kiss against her cheek.

The air between us is filled with tension. Not the good kind either, it's the awkward what-the-fuck-happens-now tension. I don't like it to say the least. I hate that this whole thing between us is putting her on edge when that's the absolute last thing I want.

I sip my coffee trying to not make it obvious that I'm staring at her. I'm trying to come up with a solution as to how to make her feel at ease around me, but she's so fucking gorgeous that it's beyond distracting. "I was wondering if you wanted to come with me to see my sister today."

I hadn't planned a trip over to my sister's place today but I have to admit, it's a pretty damn good distraction. Maybe just the one we need.

"You mean to ask, if I want to come with you to meet your sister, your brother-in-law and your baby nephew?" She looks over a me suspiciously. I wish I knew what she was thinking. She's staring holes into my naked chest but I can see that she's holding something back.

"Well, yeah. Obviously, they'll be there as well." I make light of the situation but inside I'm battling with myself. I need her to take to me, if getting alone in the car for half an hour is the only way that's going to happen - I *need* to make that happen.

"I mean, sure, if you're okay with me meeting your family." She shrugs before going back to eating her eggs.

"Yeah of course. I actually really miss seeing them every day, I didn't think I would." I can't help that my sigh sounds wistful. I do miss my family but moving in with Natasha has changed my life in more ways than I could've ever guessed. I wouldn't trade what I have now for anything in the world, I just hope I can convince Natasha that she feels the same way.

It's over an hour after breakfast when Natasha emerges from her bedroom, fresh and ready to go.

"You ready?" She asks, pulling on her coat. I stare because I don't even think she realises how she affects me, and everyone else around her. She's got this radiating aura that just captures your attention. You can try and fight it but you know you'll lose.

"You look beautiful." She's wearing jeans and a

cream sweater, her hair is neatly curled and her boots are hot as fuck. But, more than all of that, I like that she's not just dressing up for me but for my family.

"Thanks." Her smile is small, almost shy looking.

I hate it. It's a smile that says she's not used to being told just how truly remarkable she is. I hate that, but I'm working on changing it.

Despite how lovely it was to hear her say all of three words, the tension between us hasn't dissipated. I texted my sister straight after breakfast to let her know that I was heading her way. I may have hinted that I was bringing someone with me but since I can't put a label on Natasha and I just yet, I skilfully dodged all my sister's follow up questions.

After getting showered and dressed myself, I searched online for a fancy restaurant to take Natasha to tonight, assuming she agrees when I ask her. I've decided that's what I'm going to do. It's not much of a master plan but it's a start.

As soon as we step out of the building I start to doubt going out today. The clouds are covering the skies making the streets seem darker than they should be for ten in the morning. I take Natasha's hand in mine and lead her to my car. I unlock it and open the door for her to climb in.

Once we're both situated inside the car, I lock the doors and turn in my seat to face Natasha head on.

I think me locking her in must catch her off guard because her eyes fly to the door handle. "What the hell?"

"Sorry, I just don't want you running away." I pause to look at her sceptically. She looks as calm as a cucumber but her hand is frantically pulling on the interior door handle. She raises and eyebrow in question and I have to grind my teeth to keep from laughing at her sweetness. I nod towards her hand and her head swings around to look at it.

Slowly her hand drops and I continue talking, "I thought maybe we should talk, clear the air."

I start with, "About last night," but that doesn't sound right.

Natasha goes to jump in which I'm glad for, until I hear what she has to say. "I know you don't do relationships but Luke, I can't do casual sex."

"I don't expect you to, and who said I don't do relationships?" I'm pissed and eager to know who the hell has been filling her head with such negative bullshit.

"Everyone. Gabby, Kate, Ellie..." *And they'll all certainly be getting an earful later.*

"I don't want you listening to any of that." Not because it's not true, it's just not the case now. Natasha is different and I don't want her doubting us because of my past 'relationships'. "There's a difference between not doing relationships and not having been in a relationship before. I just haven't found anyone I liked enough to be in a relationship with."

"Oh. So, what does that mean?" The looks she gives me would have knocked me off my feet if I were standing. It's a look of total vulnerability, a look that warns me that the ball is in my court. This is it, that magical moment I've been waiting for to make my move.

"It means that I would really love it if you gave me a chance." I take her hand with my free one and bring it to my lips. "Tonight, we start by going out for dinner. Like a proper, just me and you, date?"

"I would love that." Her answer makes me happy. I finally press my lips against her eagerly awaiting ones. I'm not in any rush to get to my sisters and Natasha's lips are just too irresistible to deny. This is only the beginning and I thoroughly plan to enjoy every moment of our journey together, where it leads us.

Natasha has no idea how deep I'm already in, she better prepare herself for a wild ride.

# EPILOGUE
## Natasha

"Natasha?" I hear Luke call but it sounds hazy, like it's coming from far away. "What the hell? Are you okay?"

I'm a crying mess, I try to tell him but the sounds just come out all jumbled. *Oh, god.* We're going to turn into the real-life versions of Ross and Rachel.

"I can't understand what you're saying when you're crying like that. Calm down and tell me what's wrong? I promise I won't laugh, and I promise to be helpful." He pouts at me as he tries to pry the carton of cookie dough ice cream from my hands.

Luke finally tugs the ice cream free and then smiles victoriously. The smile on his face scares me more than anything else. Once I tell him, I'm going to have an up close and personal view as that annoyingly perfect smile drops off of his face, maybe forever.

"I, I'm..." I stutter. Every time I try to say it I can't help that my emotions rise all over again. I try again to calm my breathing, deep breath in, deep breath out and repeat. "I'm late."

"Well, that's nothing to cry over. There's no place important enough that deserves your tears. Grab your coat, I'll drive you."

"What?" Drive me? Oh, hang on, he didn't understand. "Luke, my period is late."

Just like I predicted, the colour drains from his face as his eyes drop to my stomach. I don't know what the fuck he's looking at it for, it's not like you'd be able to tell from the outside. If it's true, then you still wouldn't be able to tell visibly for a while yet. From my count, the very first time we'd had sex was just over two weeks.

"How?" He asks and all I can think is *Really?* I'm guessing that shows on my face as well because Luke suddenly turns away. Weeks of mind tingling mostly unprotected sex, and he wants to know how.

I don't even bother answering that. The tears start again and I can feel my body shake with my sobs. I feel like such an idiot. It's not like we went out of our way to not use protection, it just seemed to happen that way. It was almost impossible to time when Luke was going to jump on me, or when I found myself horny enough to tackle him.

The sex might've been the best beyond belief but, a baby? I can't handle that! Looking at Luke, I know we definitely can't handle that. I watch Luke pacing back and forth, the phone pressed against his ear as he freaks out to his sister.

When he finally gets off the phone he comes to kneel beside me. He looks me dead in the eye and I start to panic that little bit more because never have I seen a more serious look on Luke's face. "Have you taken a test?"

I heave a heavy sigh, "no." I don't know what I was expecting him to say but it certainly wasn't that.

"Okay, Emma suggested for *that* to be the first thing we sort out. We need to know first before we start making decisions, and freaking out about it." He's so composed as he speaks, I like it - it kind of calms my inner insanity. Maybe I jumped to conclusions, maybe Luke would make a terrific father, and he'd handle it like a boss. I still think it's way too freaking soon to be finding out though.

"I'm going to go to the store. I'll be back in a little

bit." Luke presses a kiss to my temple and then rushing out of the apartment like his ass is on fire.

I sit there, waiting, staring at nothing and at everything. I don't even know how the time passes so quickly but it does. When Luke comes back into my bedroom I haven't moved, I don't even know if I've blinked.

"Here, drink this." An open bottle of Sunny D is placed in my hand. I start to laugh; it sounds a bit manic even to my own ears. The Sunny D reminds me of a movie I watched just last month where a single teenage girl got pregnant. Of course, Luke wouldn't have known, which only makes it that much funnier.

After controlling my crazy bouts of laughter, I down the juice. I've heard that you need to pee a lot for a pregnancy test. Especially if you're using more than one.

I swallow a burp and hand the empty bottle back to Luke. "Give me ten minutes."

When Luke doesn't move from his spot beside me, I frown at him. "I'm not peeing with you sitting out here."

"Well I'm not going anywhere." He raises his eyebrow stubbornly.

"Luke!" I try but he just shakes his head.

Grunting dramatically, I pick up my phone and head into the bathroom, test clutched in hand. I close the bathroom door a little harder than necessary but make sure it's locked as well. I hit shuffle on my phone and drop my pyjama bottoms.

I'm squatting for over three songs before anything actually happens. After finishing I wash up and wait.

I feel awkward though. Am I supposed to open the door and wait with Luke? But I feel like that is for happily married couples that are desperate to have a kid.

The timer counts down on my phone but as I stare at the test I can't bring myself to go back out there and join Luke. I don't want this.

The timer buzzes and my eyes go supersonic as I will the stick to answer my burning question. I gasp in fright when I see one line appear. *Shit, what does that mean?*

I google it while still keeping an eye on the stick, afraid it's going to change its mind. I scroll through the browser on my phone not believing my eyes.

Not pregnant.

Well, thank fuck for that.

I swing open the bathroom door with the biggest grin. Luke looks up raising a questioning brow. I shake my head to his unspoken question. He's up within a second, scoping me up into his arms.

After several minutes go by we pull away, I can't

help but laugh at our exaggerated relief. I think from now on we'll be taking much better care when it comes to our sex life. While it's not the right time now, I'm not completely opposed to having kids. Just in the very distant future. Looking at Luke I'm very thankful to see that he feels the same way.

"Phew." Luke dramatically wipes the fake sweat off his brow and it makes me laugh. "Now, I think we really need some ice cream."

I look over to my bedside table where my tub is still sitting, dripping with condensation as the ice cream inside melts. "No, I mean, go out for proper ice cream."

"Sounds like a plan." I smile up at him.

"I'm really sorry I freaked out before... about the whole baby thing. I want kids but just, not right now." He explains but he really doesn't have to. We've only been together a short time. I guess at the end of the day we don't even know if we're going to end up together, let along create a family. I'm still so uncertain about us, I'm afraid every day that Luke's going to want to go back to his playboy ways.

"I get it, you don't have to explain. You don't want to be forced into anything or tied down, I really do understand. It's okay Luke." I place my hand on his arm trying to comfort him, and get out of this conversation. Right now, I don't want to focus on the future I just want to be here in the present with him.

"No, it's not. I was a complete idiot, you were just sitting there crying - I had no idea how to handle it, but I handled it wrong. But you're also wrong, I don't mind the thought of being tied down. I'd just want to tie myself to someone special before bringing a child into the world."

"Luke? It's oh-kay."

"What I'm trying to say, Natasha, is I think that you are that someone special I want to tie myself to. We've only been together such a short time but I feel it. I never thought I'd care this much about someone. Dare I say it but I think I'm starting to fall in love with you." I'm pretty sure my eyes must go as wide as saucers. I'm shell shocked.

I must be quiet for too long because he starts looking at me funny, "Natasha?"

My arms loop around his shoulders, my hands pull his neck down just enough so our lips are touching.

"I'm falling for you too." I whisper against his lips. His kiss quickly turns fevered and needy. I already know where this is going to go. My hand blindly reaches behind me to feel for my bedside table. I clasp the knob on the top drawer and tug it open. My hand digs through the contents of the drawer until I find the small foil package.

I don't think I'll be forgetting that anytime soon. Now let the fun begin.

## The End

# AUTHOR'S Note

Dear Readers,

For me this has probably been the hardest story to write (with life getting in the way) but it was Natasha's charisma that helped me along. The tale of Natasha and Luke was short but sweet, it's not over though. The next instalment of the Vibrations Collection – Capture Me – will be releasing soon. For everyone who has read and loved Save Me, I hope this lived up to your expectations.

I have a number of books releasing this year so keep an eye out for them. And, as always, if you're interested in being kept updated on what I'm working on and my new releases head over to my social media pages or simply email me.

I'd like to thank all my readers for taking a chance on Hold Me. If you did enjoy it, I welcome you to write a review on Amazon/Goodreads/Bookbub to promote the book to other curious readers. Plus, I love hearing your thoughts and opinions!

Until next time,
    Chelsea xo

# OTHER TITLES BY
## *Chelsea McDonald*

The Accord Series:

Lunar Accord, Book 1

Mortal Accord, Book 2 (Coming October 2019)

Vibrations Novella Series:

Save Me

Hold Me

Capture Me (Coming 2019)

Armstrong Lovers Series:

Claimed (Kennedy & Nathaniel)

# CONTACT THE

*You can find Chelsea on Facebook:*
*https://www.facebook.com/AuthorCMcDonald*

*Instagram:*
*https://www.instagram.com/AuthorCMcDonald*

*Twitter:*
*http://www.twitter.com/AuthorCMcDonald*

*Or, contact her directly by email:*
*authorcmcdonald@gmail.com*

43767927R00070

Printed in Poland
by Amazon Fulfillment
Poland Sp. z o.o., Wrocław